# of Bees and Bats
# of Crocodiles
and Cats

With illustrations by
Jennifer Ker

Foreword

For some years I have been writing verses, mainly about animals, for my grandchildren, and, as they have grown older, they seem to have enjoyed them even more than when very young. They, together with friends, have been suggesting that I publish them, hence this wee book. My motivation has been to entertain and I have deliberately fought shy of more conventional children's styles which is why, perhaps, these verses may be attractive to a broader age group. I am wont to suggest that they appeal to the child in all of us!

In memory of Billy Jack, a true Olympian and my lifelong friend.

Illustrations by Jennifer Ker, Billy's granddaughter

Content

Timothy

Timothy toad was very slim,
there was no way of fattening him.
His mother tried, but tried in vain,
not one ounce of fat he'd gain!
She fed him on such tasty bites
as grubs and flies and sweet termites;
all his friends could not deny it,
his was a very special diet!

Whilst his friends all grew quite stout,
Timothy toad was missing out!
Untoad like in his slim sleek form,
no winter fat to keep him warm;
more worrying, his mother said,
no slim line toad would ever wed,
he would be always by her side,
not for him a webbed foot bride!

He was quite happy for all that,
without ambition to be fat;
and, being slim and fit, you see,
won all the games quite easily!
He played with his much plumper friends,
who found it hard to run round bends,
to leap as high, or run so free,
but bore no sign of jealousy.

One day when they were all at play,
on a bright and sunny day,
without a thought of danger then,
they played as outlaws and kings men.
So caught up in their game, alas,
they failed to see the waving grass,
had they been rather more awake
they may have sooner seen the snake!

Sinclair had been asleep nearby,
their noise awoke him to espy
some rather appetising food,
a shortish slither from where he stood,
or rather lay, is better put,
since snakes have neither leg nor foot,
for them no handicap, indeed,
a snake may slither at great speed.
A plump young toad would not outlast
a Sinclair out to break his fast!

He slithered noiseless, eyes alight;
as, unaware of their dire plight,
the young toads played on, quite carefree,
running and jumping merrily.
As Sinclair slithered, a tiny stone
became dislodged, and, it alone
turned the toads to where the snake
lay poised, and was about to break
the cover from wherein he lay
and, mouth wide open, seize his prey!

Sinclair stopped, the toads surprised
turned and saw him, mesmerised.
The safety of the stream now lay,
for the toads, too far away,
and though they knew he could not swim,
none, they knew could outspeed him.
Timothy toad, with brave intent,
though Sinclair's gaze did not relent,
cried out to all the others "hide!"
and, turning, took one massive stride,
then, before Sinclair understood,
ran off quickly, towards the wood.

Sinclair curled his tail, and then
slithering quickly once again,
raced to catch the little toad
before the river, by the road,
could intervene and let his prey,
live to fight another day!
Sinclairs slithering was slick,
but he had never met so quick
a toad, whose legs could speed
so very quickly, and, indeed,
as Sinclair very shortly found,
was quicker than he, over the ground.
Then soon before them; what a sight,
the river, seen in sheer delight,
toad plunged in with little splash,
Sinclair stopped and muttered "dash!"

Meanwhile the other toads had found
a tiny track, which took them round
the forest edge, and , once they breached
a hedge, the river safely reached.
Great was the rejoicing then,
when all were safely home again.
Timothy toad, a hero proud,
was hugged and kissed and cheered aloud!
Much favoured now by all the lasses,
they come to him for swimming classes!

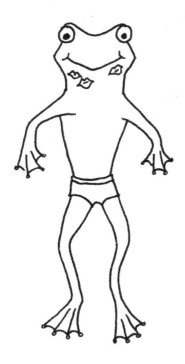

The Pincushion

Molly Prichard was shortsighted,
glasses perched on end of nose.
Inevitably sitting sewing
patchwork quilts where'er she goes.
In the summer, in the garden,
dreaming gently in the sun,
fingers slowing in their stitching
of a quilt, not long begun.

Henrietta was a hedgehog,
thought quite plain by all the rest;
none of them had ever told her,
she was too sweet, one of the best
and gentle creatures one could ever hope to find
but, just like every other hedgehog,
in bright sunlight, almost blind.

Sniffing for a tasty morsel,
she crossed the lawn that afternoon,
not aware of Molly Prichard,
then, came upon her chair quite soon.
Stopping, sniffing, for a moment,
Henrietta sat so still
beside the chair where Molly Prichard
quietly pursued her skill.

Molly Prichard's head was nodding,
sleep was not so far away,
and as her eyelids started closing
the quilt upon her lap did lay.
Her hand dropped down, where Henrietta
sat silently beside the chair,
felt the quills of Henrietta,
thought it her pincushion there!

Gently Molly set her needle
into Henriettas back!
Henrietta jumped up, startled,
crossed the lawn, and found the track
that led to where the other hedgehogs
played, or lazed, beneath the trees.
When they saw her and the needle
said - why can't we have one of these?

As the sun shone, so the needle
glinted, sparkled, in the light,
and later, after darkness fell,
glowed liquid silver in moonlight.
Other hedgehogs came to woo her,
sought to make of her a wife,
Molly Prichard never knew
how she'd changed Henrietta's life.

The Trap

As darkness fell, the stars came out,
moonlight bathed the town
in silver, gold and purple,
all the colours of a crown.
A silence fell upon it,
and, in one rather special house,
the sound that broke the silence
was, the patter of a mouse!

A tiny little fieldmouse,
not really very old,
had found its way into the kitchen
to shelter from the cold.
It was truely unaccustomed
to surroundings such as these,
but soon its nose detected
the quite distinctive smell of cheese!

The tiny furry creature
stood so still, then sniffed the air;
the scent was at its strongest
in a corner by a chair.
Its tiny nose aquiver
the mouse scurried across the floor
and saw the tasty morsel,
a month's supply or more!

Unaccustomed to a kitchen
with its pots its pans and like,
the mouse felt no suspicion
that the cheese was on a spike,
or, that a spring was tightly coiled
to hold a metal flap.
Our country friend was unaware
it was a deadly trap!

The cheese was farmhouse cheddar,
mature and rich - the best
the tiny mouse had ever seen,
she would take it to her nest.
How then was she to move it,
such a monstrous piece of cheese?
She would call upon her closest friends
to share, in times like these.
But first, a tiny little taste,
a nibble just to prove
this was indeed a worthy cheese,
a special feast to move!

She stood upon the platform
where the cheese lay, by that chair,
and, stretching out her little neck -
at once became aware
of noises in the background,
of movement in the house,
she scurried quickly out of sight,
that timid little mouse.

The owner of the house was one
Nathaniel by name,
a large man, with an appetite
to match his portly frame!
It often was his habit,
in the small hours of the night,
when he was feeling peckish,
to go down and have a bite.

Thus it was, the noise he made
in coming down the stair,
although not much, it was enough
to make our mouse aware -
and, as she watched from hiding,
Nathaniel made his way
to the refrigerator,
where his intended nibbles lay.

He forgot that, in the evening,
before he closed the door,
he had set that wicked mousetrap
by the corner on the floor!
As he walked across the kitchen,
his foot disturbed the trap,
his toe, peeking through worn slippers
did activate the snap!!

With a shout that woke his neighbours,
Nathaniel hopped and cried,
then quickly ran back up to bed,
for it was warm inside.
Not really understanding
her close brush with destiny,
our tiny furry friend invited
all her friends for tea!

The Three Legged Cat

I had never heard of a tripod cat,
until, one day upon the mat
at the home of an old and treasured chum
I saw a cat, whose total sum
of legs amounted to just three,
a fact which rather puzzled me.
How did you lose a leg? I asked
the cat, who answered, expression masked
by a look of quite complete disdain,
"do I have to answer that again?"

"It began a long, long, time ago,
I am a royal cat, you know,
and a noble feline predecessor
was pet to Edward, the confessor!"
Not always the most caring king,
his barons fought like anything
to sieze the throne and all its power,
in short, they were a frightful shower!

11

One night some barons quietly crept
to where the monarch soundly slept,
Edward and his faithful cat,
curled up beside him, on the mat.
The cat of course, with hearing keen
awoke, before upon the scene
the barons came to take the king,
which would have been a dreadful thing!

Leaping to his four deft paws,
he ran toward the door, because
he sensed the menace in the air,
and, leaping nimbly on a chair,
threw himself from chair to bed
landing on that kingly head!

The royal personage awoke,
and, thrusting his arm out, at a stroke
swept the cat from off the bed,
while, at his waking, the barons fled!
Alas! - the cat was not unscathed,
a badly injured leg he waved,
somewhat limply in the air.

Realising this affair
had been aborted by his cat,
the king immediately said, that
this animal, by my decree
from henceforth shall a royal be!
That night was not without its cost;
the injured leg - alas - was lost.
Thus it is, to this, from that,
I am a royal tripawed cat!

Millicent's Great Adventure

Millicent was never very happy in the rain,
a tiny mouse of rather gentle habit.
Out in the sun she'd run and play, happy as anything,
with all her friends, like vole and shrew and rabbit.
But when it rained that tiny mouse,
would have to run and hide,
her fine brown coat all ruffled in the breeze,
and, should the rainfall catch her before she got inside,
she would catch a cold and cough and sniff and sneeze!
Her mother always told her,
when she saw dark clouds above,
to be sure to find a cozy hiding place,
there to remain until the rain completely died away,
curled up and dry within her resting place.
One day, as brightly shone the sun, high in the sky above,
she skipped and hopped and jumped so happily,
unaware that danger lay not far from where she played,
for a sparrowhawk, quite still, sat in a tree!

Silently he spread his wings and slipped into the air
and, soaring upward in the sun warmed sky,
the tiny hopping figure of a plump young mouse appeared
within the compass of his beady eye!
Millicent, still unaware of peril high above,
continued dancing through the field of hay;
skipping along and singing, quite the happiest of mice;
content and smiling on that sun filled day.

Millicent danced, watched closely now,
by black and beady eye,
as, sparrowhawk began to circle round;
a moment now and he would swoop,
with talons spread out wide,
then would he snatch his prey up from the ground!

Just as he began to plan this appetising meal,
a cloud slid, very gently, past the sun;
remembering her mother's words
hide quickly should it rain
without a pause the mouse began to run!
The hawk pulled in its wings and dropped
speedily down to earth
then used its wings to glide at such a rate
that, quickly though young Millicent
could scamper through the grass,
it seemed that she must meet a dreadful fate!
Just as the hawk reached out to grasp
the panting ball of fur,
she slithered, sideways, down a long steep furrow;
and, tumbling over, breathless now
with energy all spent,
she rolled into a rabbit's empty burrow!

It was only some time later, as a brisk and drying wind,
had blown the clouds away and she could see
the danger she, unknowing had so narrowly escaped,
sitting, waiting, watching, in a tree!
She dozed off, knowing very soon,
his hunger would ensure
that he would fly to seek some other prey,
and, when he did, she would be safe,
but she must wait till then
to leave, and homeward make her careful way.
Patiently she looked out from the burrow, safe and warm
saw the rain slide from his plumage brown,
she wondered how he sat so still, so unperturbed and calm
whilst all the rain had been cascading down?
At last the hawk, impatient, as his hunger now increased,
raised his majestic wings and flew away
to scan the fields and woodlands, hills and valleys too,
for he had eaten little, all that day.

Millicent scampered homewards
where her mother did await
to wrap her in her warm and welcome arms,
and, listen to her daughter tell the tale of her escape,
and of the sparrowhawk and her alarms.
She told of how she wondered
how that haughty bird could fly
when heavy rain made all things damp and wet,
the water sliding off him, none of it soaking in,
a sight that Millicent would not forget!

That night her mother crept out
from the nest by light of moon,
and, moving swiftly through the grass and sedge,
found what she was seeking,
some feathers brown and green,
lying, quite discarded, by a hedge.
Carefully she dragged them home,
this took some little time,
but, once she had them home, began to sew,
so busy was she that she knew
when morning came around
only when the cock began to crow!

Millicent rubbed the sleep out of her eyes
and raised her head,
saw, with wonder, as the daylight broke,
lying by her bedside
made from feathers brown and green,
a beautifully hand embroidered cloak!
Now Millicent need never fear
the clouds that harbour rain,
never need again to sneeze or cough.
With her new cloak around her
she can brave the fiercest storm
and, laughing, watch the drops of rain run off!

The Olympian

Timothy toad was a champion jumper
could jump higher and farther than all of his chums.
After school playing games he was always the first
to be chosen, but hopeless at English and sums!
His mother and father were so disappointed;
of what use was jumping when making his way
in this world, he would need education -
but playing and jumping just filled every day!

One day by the river, while watching his friends
diving and swimming and drifting about,
he espied a large pike lying still in the water,
he leapt to his feet and he started to shout!
His friends did not hear him, intent on their playing,
the pike drifted closer, now soon to be fed!
Timothy watched, his tiny heart pounding,
then leapt from the river bank on the pike's head!

The fish, suddenly startled, dived down in the river,
while young Timothy swam, rather quickly away!
His friends gathered round him, now aware
of the danger, cried out
Bravo! young Timothy Hip Hip Hooray!
Now his mother and father are proud of their Timothy,
his jumping the subject of so much esteem.
Now they are planning to honour young Timothy,
as a member of next toads' olympic jump team!

Eggsactly

Mhairi was a hen who laid
eggs of brightest blue,
it really was a puzzle,
what was she to do?
A quite well meaning cockerel
said, "no eating in betweens -
simply three good meals a day-
and lots and lots of greens!"
He knew little about colours,
that well intentioned fellow,
the next time Mhairi laid an egg
it was a bold, bright, sunshine yellow!

The Silver Buckle

Jenny lost the silver buckle,
from her shoe it fell one night.
She looked and looked but could not find it,
though the moon shone clear and bright.
Silent tears began to gather -
how she loved those shiny shoes -
till she heard from out the woodland,
gentle, soft, TOOwit TOOwoos!
Alighting on a branch above her,
lowered brows would seem to scowl,
Then a voice said "may I help you?"
and she saw it was an owl!
Blessed with wonderous sight in darkness,
the buckle found, much to her glee,
Jenny smiled, and, saying "thank you"
asked the owl back home to tea!

Emily

Emily, a honeybee, living in a hive,
normally worked from nine till five.
But, with the pollen harvest due,
overtime was needed too.
She smiled, sighed gently to herself
and lay on her allotted shelf,
and, counting pollen as we count sheep,
in time, she nodded off to sleep.

Sometime in the night perturbed,
she woke, to find her sleep disturbed.
She listened, with hearing quite profound
to what seemed like a clicking sound.
Awakened now she gently crept
past where her fellow workers slept
and, as the moonlight filled the entry
to the hive, she saw the sentry.
A member of the upper classes,
now filled with honey and molasses,
this night, his watch, he could not keep,
but lay aside quite fast asleep!

Quietly she passed him where he lay,
and, without undue delay
she flew above a nearby thicket
and, there it was she saw the cricket!

Coloured a pleasing green and yellow,
this long legged, rather gangling fellow,
hummed and clicked as in a trance,
whilst up and down the grass he pranced.
She watched, for it was so entrancing,
then, realised that he was dancing!

Excited by this new pursuit
she vowed that she would follow suit.
Alighting near him on the grass
she tried to follow, but alas!
her legs were short, try as she might,
she made a somewhat sorry sight.
The cricket stopped at her intrusion,
tried not to laugh at this illusion,
in all his life he knew that he,
had never seen a dancing bee!
He took her gently by the wing,
and, tenderly as anything,
he slowly took her through the paces,
and, looking at their smiling faces
it would be clear to anyone
that dancing truely can be fun!

Unknown to the tiny pair,
the queen bee's cousin took the air,
and, droning softly o'er the thicket
saw Emily dancing with the cricket.
A worker bee out having fun?
Clearly something must be done.
So, with a quite disdainful glance,
as, unaware on went the dance;
the queen's close kin turned round to dive
true as an arrow to the hive.

The queen, a rather stout and wheezy
bee, had never found it easy
to fly around, or even glide,
for, with her weight she would subside
puffing and blowing to the ground.
Thus, worker bees were summoned round
and, not without much hue and cry,
would lift her back, to where she'd lie
and, if the weather bright and sunny,
soothe her aches and pains with honey!

On hearing her good cousin's news
the queen of bees began to muse,
saying nothing for a while,
unpleasantly, began to smile.
Then, as her anger did increase,
she summoned up the bee police!
Instructing them to follow her,
her tiny wings began to whirr
and, assisted by the nearest pair
the queen and police took to the air!

The police, I must say, hand on heart,
all looked extremely neat and smart;
black hats sat on each little head,
with buttoned tunics in bright red.
A pair of orange yellow britches
were tied around with purple stitches.
As fine a group as you could find
except, they left the queen behind!
Puffing and panting, I can't deny it
she truely should be on a diet!

At last they came to where our dancers
were boldly stepping out the lancers
quite unaware, it should be said,
of trouble looming overhead.
Feeling even more enraged,
the queen, in anger, disengaged
from her two helpers; would you know,
and fell down to the earth below!
As she landed, sad to say,
she fell upon poor Emily!

"Oh! Majesty" she heard her say,
"have I offended in any way?"
The queen replied "No! not at all,
it was kind of you to break my fall,
now while I watched you from the sky,
I thought that dancing, was what I
would much enjoy,-it would deflate
my present -slight - surplus of weight!
So, come my little ones and show
me just how these dance steps should go"
The queen arose from where she fell,
as did sweet Emily as well,
and, to this day, those little creatures
are well respected dancing teachers!

Pigs in my Life

There are not many pigs that are pink,
bright pink, around seven I think.
Young Clarence was one of that hue;
though it would be worse had he been blue.
Bright bright pink, that's the colour he was,
and, some animals laughed, just because
they had never seen his sort before,
but his mother just loved him the more.

During bright sunny days on the farm,
when the wind dropped and it became warm,
all the sensible pigs found some shade,
and, sensibly in it they stayed.
Not young Clarence, much too full of joy
I suppose, and like any young boy,
be he pig, duck, or dog - or like us,
he would wish to play games, then he'd fuss
around those sleeping pigs, just to try
and make one of them open an eye,
whereupon they would grudgingly see
a pink pig saying "come play with me!"

There are not many pigs that are green,
only one in my lifetime I've seen.
Now I know there are people I've heard
who say to me don't be absurd
but, I won't give a jot or a fig,
my friend Andrew's a green flying pig!

Whenever I have a sore head,
or I'm lying unwell in my bed,
I hear knocking on my window pane,
and, it's Andrew to cheer me again.
Or, if I feel lonely and sad,
if there's not too much fun to be had,
he is there, at the drop of a hat,
and I truely am glad about that.
My friend Andrew, the children's delight,
and, like them, I can see him alright.

To my knowledge, this statement is true,
there are no pigs at all that are blue,
bright blue, blackish blue, there are some,
but being so dark, they don't come
into that intimate set
of pigs I shall never forget.
From my pigs pink and green I'll ne'er part
but then, I'm a romantic at heart!

Tongue Tied

"Look at the length of your tongue!"
they all laughed,
as the anteater licked up some honey.
A family of bears,
with wide brown eyed stares,
certainly thought it was funny!
Until, one dark night
when returning home late,
father bear dropped their one front door key.
It lay where it fell,
in a rather deep well,
by the light of the moon they could see.
"Now, look at the lenght of my tongue!"
cried the anteater,
how he licked up the key I can't say.
But he did, and the cheers
that rang in his ears,
are with him to this very day!

Bella

Bella the butterfly's wings were pure white,
how she longed to be yellow or blue.
Though they reflected the sun's early light,
she yearned for a colourful hue.
Oh! how she envied her friends in the sun,
who were red, purple, blue and deep yellow,
and, truth to tell, a particular one,
an excitingly bold, bright, young fellow!
Sadly she flew in the crisp morning air,
till a cloud drifted over the sun,
and the patter of raindrops was heard everywhere;
she looked round, for somewhere to run.

Bedraggled by raindrops, she staggered in flight,
'till a shaft of bright light split the sky,
and a wonderful rainbow of colours, so bright,
arched above, and she through it did fly.
She glimpsed her reflection, in water below
and she hung in the air in surprise,
now, on her wings, rainbow colours did glow
and pure happiness shone from her eyes!

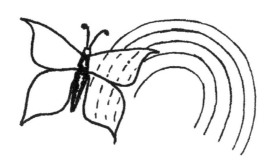

Bathtime

"Wash me first!" cried Fennella Foot, archly.
"No! Wash me!" cried out Nobby the knee.
"I really think I
should be first !" said Tim thigh,
"No!" said hand, " it should really be me,
for I lather the soap!"
Said an arm, "you've no hope
I control you with such great precision."
Then the mouth smiled, and said,
"it just has to be head,
because he makes the final decision!"

Sinclair and the Bats

Bats are nocturnal, which means to say,
they fly by night, and not by day.
They play, and hunt for food to keep
them satisfied, then fall asleep.
Another habit of the bat
is rather strange, and it is that
when they are sleeping, please don't frown,
you will find them hanging upside down!

They live in groups, or families,
preferring attic rooms to trees,
and, into one such colony
a tiny bat was born one day.
They called the newborn Christopher,
a tiny ball of skin and fur,
but, very soon, as time went by,
he learned, from mum, to hunt and fly.

He learned quite quickly, but strange to say,
when night was gone, and came the day,
he caused confusion, I expect,
while they hung down, he stood erect!
He did try hanging like the rest,
but, when he did, his little chest
began to hurt, and, as he said,
he felt so dizzy in the head!
So, on his perch, asleep he stood,
whilst other bats thought that he would,
when he was sleeping, perhaps fall,
but no, he slept there, upright, tall!

30

Sinclair the snake had several chums,
and, smiling, as he licked his gums
said, now put on your party hats,
I've found a colony of bats!
Now, snakes are not fussy what they eat,
alas! no veg, it's mainly meat.
That's why some people do declare
they have no white teeth or curly hair!
I don't know very much of that,
but do know they are fond of bat!
Sinclair's friends all looked delighted
that they had all been thus invited
to share his secret - so this bunch
of serpents all set off to lunch!

They slithered off to where there stood
an ancient barn, just where the wood
grew thinner and a little space
had been cleared, for the Dawson's place.
They slithered close, and, at the back,
Sinclair had noticed quite a crack
between two boards, and, not too thin
to stop a snake from slithering in!

Sinclair whispered, "over there,
in that far corner, but do take care
to make no sound or we must run,
or rather slither, because a gun,
is never very far away
from Dawsons hand, so, do not delay,
if you are ready, follow me,
enjoy your meal; Bon Appetit!"

As Sinclair neared the sleeping bats,
a shaft of sunlight through some slats,
threw Christopher's shadow on the wall,
which magnified him six feet tall!
The snakes were terrified by this,
and, letting out a frightened hiss
turned, and slithered quickly back
the way they came, to find the crack.
Alas! a swishing tail then caught
around a large, brown, earthen pot,
brought it crashing to the floor,
and Dawson, gun in hand, to door!

They barely made it to the wood,
Dawson saw them from where he stood,
he took a shot, but hurriedly,
hit or miss? He could not see.
But Sinclair did! He could not fail
to feel the buckshot in his tail.
Later, with pain and swelling gone,
a vegetarian from now on!

A Friend in Need

The dunlin paused and slowly raised his hat
to where the oystercatcher sadly sat.
Small tears were softly falling down his cheeks,
he had not caught an oyster for two weeks.
He was not sad for hunger's not what ails,
he had been satisfied by worms and snails,
No, the reason for him feeling sad and blue
was he said, "that oyster catching's what I do!"

The dunlin, a most kind and gentle bird,
was troubled by these soulful words he heard,
and, there and then, decided 'midst the kelp,
that he would find a way, his friend to help.
Now some may find a winkle not quite nice,
nor the creature you would turn to for advice,
but, to seek him out the dunlin made a start,
he knew his looks belied a tender heart!

When he heard the news, the winkle gave a frown,
there were some stories coming from the town.
The king and all his court had come to stay
and, featured oysters on the menu every day.
The winkle said 't was better if we did
enlist the help of Sid and Sammy squid,
or, should the squids be busy; never fuss,
I'm quite well known to Olive Octopus!

That very day the cooks came to the shore,
again to collect oysters by the score.
Then, stopping on the sand began to blink,
The water was not blue, but black as ink!
They raced back to the king to break the news
that, clearly, oysters there they could not use.

"Black Oysters!" cried the king, quite sorely tried,
"that will not do! that will not do!" he cried!
"Black oysters will upset our red corpuscles,
we must make up with winkles, welks and mussles!"
The rising tide soon cleared the inky pool.
Sid And Sammy scampered back to school.
The winkle smiled, and, nodding his wise head,
saw nothing had disturbed the oyster bed!

The dunlin ran to tell his doleful friend,
that, all his troubles now were at an end.
Then, proudly, at the oystercatcher's side,
saw his friend restore professional pride!

A Prickly Situation

A hedgehog at best is an uneasy guest,
at a party, with coloured balloons.
On his quills they all burst;
but that isn't the worst,
when it comes to them singing the tunes.
They all sing so off key,
that between you and me,
the other guests cover their ears,
but they sing with such verve,
that no one has the nerve
to be rude, and reduce them to tears!

BUT - after each DO -
between me and you,
a hedgehog's the guest the host likes,
instead of a broom,
they roll round the room,
and pick everything up on their spikes!

Sinclair and the Lilypond

Timothy toad had always been
quite musically inclined
to form a choir of toads and frogs
was foremost in his mind.
From time to time a few of them
would practice in a glade
or, when at home with groups of friends
their talents would parade.
Then finally, the dream to which
our young friend would aspire
was realised, as twelve of them
agreed to form a choir!
Now, you and I might fail to find
the noise they made endearing,
but, to a frog, the croaks and groans
they uttered in that clearing
were sheer delight, a joy to all
and much appreciated
by young and old, despite their repetoire
being somewhat dated!

For Christmas day they had arranged
a festive great event
to present the choir dramatically
was toad's avowed intent,
so, for their last rehearsal
everyone could see he had
gathered all the choir, mid-pond
upon a lily pad!

With moon and stars above them,
the shimmering pond below,
everyone agreed this was
a very special show.
Came the night, the singers reached
the centre of the pool
and, being christmas, all the children
now quite free from school
were allowed to stay up late to hear
the music being sung,
they joined their parents at the pool
the old folk with the young!

Now Sinclair, sleeping in a shady hollow in the grass,
was awakened by the singing, and, not musical alas!
was feeling rather peevish, so rudely to be woken,
and, as his tail swished to and fro it was a certain token
of his anger, his annoyance, what a liberty to take,
they should be taught
that there is naught
as fearsome as a snake!

Sinclair slithered noiselessly
to where the toads had gathered
singing, quite oblivious
of Sinclair who had lathered
himself into a fearful rage
although this righteous stand
had more to do with having had
no christmas dinner planned!

He watched, unnoticed by the pond
and saw quite quickly that
the lily pads were plentiful
on which the toads all sat.
They looked secure, thought Sinclair
no great swimmer he,
they'd bear his weight, then might he bear
some plump toads home for tea!

So silently, and slowly,
Sinclair edged his serpent way,
out upon the water
on some lily leaves did sway.
They held him as he lay there
in anticipatory state,
until, at last, from head to tail
they held the snake's full weight!
He lay there, eyeing up his prey
"the fattest first, I think,"
he smiled, and as he licked his lips
Sinclair began to sink!

Now though a serpent, Sinclair
was no serpent of the sea,
and, as I said before, alas!
this snake no swimmer he!
Thus it was, that, as he sank
and knew not what to do,
swallowing lots of water,
turned a delicate shade of blue!

Timothy toad and all his friends
now saw his sorry plight,
as, gently, yet with dignity
Sinclair sank from sight.

A cheer began, but was cut short
and soon became a frown,
as all the frogs and toads could see
that he might even drown.
Timothy toad, first to react
cried "quickly to his tail!"
The others rushed to aid him
lest the rescue effort fail.

Struggling and slipping,
they all pulled so lustily;
until at last, poor Sinclair lay
quite from the water free.
Eyes closed upon his back he lay
looking rather stout,
Tomothy then knew what to do
they must pump his stomach out!

He lead the way and others followed
leaping up and down,
upon poor Sinclairs bloated tum
he even yet might drown!
Laughing now, as they all jumped
to pump the water out,
From Sinclair's open mouth there sprang,
an arching water spout!

The younger toads and frogs ran up
to gambol in the spray,
they later said, there never was
a more fun filled christmas day!
At last they heard a hissing
and a rather strangled cough,
all the toads and frogs stopped jumping up
and all jumped off!
Sinclair, to his credit
with some presence and some grace,
slithered soggily, and damply
from that most unhappy place!
Has Sinclair learned his lesson?
I beg you keep this quiet
as far as I'm aware he is on
a vegetarian diet!

Toothsome

Sadie was a crocodile,
with a quite beguiling smile,
but, as her teeth shone in the sun,
she terrified most everyone!
Though longing to be loved by all,
the jungle creatures, great and small,
would run away, with frightened cry
when they saw Sadie floating by.

One day a nasty pack of dogs
had trapped a young deer, by some logs.
Hearing their yapping, Sadie swam
across the river by the dam,
and to the deer's intense relief,
she smiled, and showed off all her teeth!
The dogs turned, barked, with yelps and squeals,
the whole pack taking to their heels.
When the young deer had told the herd
of her escape, upon my word,
Sadie, amidst a heartfelt cheer,
became an honorary deer!

Stardom

The sight of a cricket, all gangly legs,
dancing in time to a band of young frogs,
was apt to cause laughter in anyone passing,
and a group of young ants, sitting near on some logs.
A moth, passing by could not possibly fail,
to see him; and smile at his plight;
and, being kind hearted, she turned in mid air,
poor young cricket; I must put him right.
She alighted beside him, and taking her cue
from the band, she started to dance,
and, while they were dancing, a TV producer
happened to pass, quite by chance.
Taken aback by what he was seeing,
and, astonished by such grace and charm,
now, you may see, on TV , if your lucky,
come dancing on animal farm!

Recharged

Willie was a glowworm; no denying that;
but, alas! poor Willie, his battery was flat!
He did his best, puffed up his chest,
but, unglowing, there he sat!
One night, at play, in a wood nearby
some frightening noises made him cry.
Then, in that wood, near where he stood,
a figure caught his eye!
Nearer it came, then closer still,
what a dreadful fright he had!
What a relief it was to find
that it was Willie's dad!

He had come out, since it was dark
to where his young son played.
He knew young Willie's light was out,
and that worried him, he said.
Willie clasped his father's hand;
such happiness he showed,
shouting aloud and laughing, as
he danced along the road!
and, while he danced,
skipped and pranced,
he GLOWED, GLOWED and GLOWED!

Hippocritical

The young hippopotamus
found life so monotonous;
with the sun rising high
in the African sky
in the heat of the day.
But, as a dutiful daughter
went down to the water,
with her parents to stay,
in the heat of the day.

Young Alfie the crocodile,
with a bright, ever ready smile,
lazed in the river,
but, awake to whatever
should drift his way,
in the heat of the day.

Petronella the paraqueet,
often so indiscrete,
but, truth be told,
with a heart of pure gold,
did on a branch sway,
in the heat of the day.
No longer lumbering,
but now deeply slumbering
the hippos together
in the very hot weather,
slept time away;
in the heat of the day.

Alfie, quite lazily
made his way mazily,
through the reeds of the stream,
and, with eyes all agleam
spotted his prey,
in the heat of the day.
Closer, he drifted,
head slightly lifted
the better to see
the young hippo; she
was looking inviting,
a meal quite exciting,
some moments away!
in the heat of the day.

A baboon, with some ease,
had swung through the trees
and, a bough roughly shaken
did Petronella awaken,
to cry out "here I say!"
in the heat of the day.
At that gaudy bird's squawk,
though in parakeet talk,
all the hippopotamii
opened just one eye,
to see Alfie, teeth flashing.
Father hippo came dashing
through the water to where,
young Alfie did dare,
to lie in the water
contemplating his daughter,
as delicious entree
in the heat of the day!

With one mighty blow
from his foot, he laid low
young Alfie, who fled
with a very sore head,
a lump underneath,
and some very loose teeth,
in the heat of the day!
Now prone to be quiet,
much changed is his diet.
From then on, truth to say,
in the heat of the day.

Fairyland

Charlotte, a lovely dormouse,
lay dreaming on the grass,
when, by her side, a fairy prince,
most handsome, chanced to pass.
He took her by her paw, and smiled,
then they began to fly,
together they went soaring
to his castle in the sky!

Beyond the clouds the sun shone
ever brighter on her cheek,
and, in wonder, looking around her,
did not dare to speak!
Castle towers and spires arose
from every cloud below,
in gold, in crimson, red and silver,
colours all aglow!

He led her to a castle,
bathed in glorious light,
its towers, and its walls were all
of ivory; pure white.
He led her to a turret,
where she stood in complete awe,
he, never ceasing for a moment
to hold the tiny paw.

Below her, in the courtyard,
was a smile on every face.
"Oh! Prince she cried please tell me
I need never leave this place?"
The prince smiled yet again and said;
"if you are good and kind
this realm of light and happiness
will live on in your mind.
You only have to close your eyes
and smile within your heart,
and, from this fairy wonderland
you may never part."

He led her from that castle
to the earth below,
laying her gently on the grass
before, with movements slow,
he blew a kiss, then, flew away
beyond where she could see,
then she awoke to find that there
was pumpkin pie for tea!

Boom

Bitterns boom,
It's perfectly true
that, the sound they make
to me and you,
seems to be a deep and doleful tone
unique to bitterns, and them alone.

To be a bittern's neighbour, can
be somewhat disturbing
and, rather than
enjoying the countryside around,
"For Sale" signs proliferate
I found!
Those who choose to stay I find
are of the older, deafer kind!

Thus it is, and sad to say,
a lonely breed of birds are they,
thus, if you hear a bittern, do
pause, and pass a word or two,
because, I am sure,
what e're you say,
YOU could make a bittern's day!

Old One Eye

The one eyed dog sat, looking
quite ferocious in the garden.
Other cats and dogs, on passing, said
"I beg your pardon!"
Those other animals, with him,
had reached an understanding;
politely giving way to him,
and, being undemanding.
It had been thus for quite some time,
several years I think,
when a new arrival at number seven
began to stretch and blink.
A grey'ish, white'ish sort of dog,
and of only middling size,
perhaps a cross bred terrier,
with mischief in his eyes.

He left his house that morning
to survey the neighbourhood,
and find some cats to chase
or dogs to bully if he could.
He did not fail to notice
where old One Eye proudly sat,
but this stranger quite ignored him,
and a grave mistake was that.
The one eyed dog moved slowly,
menace in every pace,
the stranger stopped and saw that
only one eye was in place.

He backed away, as old One Eye
began a fearful growl
and felt himself a mite perturbed
by his dark threatening scowl!
The stranger turned, and made his way
thoughtfully to his home.

He would never let Old One Eye
dictate where he could roam.
"A one eyed dog" he reasoned
can see only from one side,
and, if he crept behind him,
then, noiselessly could slide
upsides him on his blind side,
before he was aware,
then bark and give his leg a nip,
to give him such a scare!

Later in the day the stranger
started his wicked plan.
Along an adjoining crescent
the stranger quickly ran.
The one eyed dog sat, motionless,
looking straight ahead,
the stranger laughed; but quietly,
"just as I thought" he said!
Down on his haunches, inching forward,
making not a sound
the stranger, ever nearer to old One Eye
made his ground.

He came within a foot or so,
and, when ready to attack
old One Eye whipped around
and sent him reeling on his back!

With pride and spirit injured.
he retreated to his lair.
What special magic sense had warned
old One Eye he was there?
That old dog started smiling
looking forward, one eye wide,
reflecting all around him
in the window on the other side!

The Faerie Piper

Hamish played the bagpipes, rather badly,
and lived outside Dunvegan on his own.
A very friendly fellow, but, quite sadly
his friends just could not stand the frightful drone.
They encouraged him to take up the piano,
the fiddle, the accordion, the comb!
But, Hamish, being Scottish to his bootstraps,
in the pipes had found his spiritual home.
Thus it was, in solitary splendour,
bedecked in highland jacket, kilt, and hose,
Hamish practised,
unaware of his shortcomings,
and the tuneless caterwaulings that arose.

Morag was a kind and gentle woman,
very much respected in the town,
but, even she admitted to her neighbour,
the noise that Hamish made quite got her down!
Sleeping was a problem for her children,
as Hamish made his living from his farm,
he could only really practice in the evenings,
waking all the younger folk in some alarm!

This can't go on, said Morag, one fine Tuesday,
as she walked out on the hill far from the noise,
it is driving all the villagers demented,
especially the younger girls and boys.

The sun was setting, and as Morag wandered
lazily and gazing fondly round,
upon the gentle breeze from 'cross the river
she clearly heard the highland bagpipes' sound!
This time she knew that it could not be Hamish,
since the playing was quite expert, full, and grand,
Morag longed to see who played the pipes so finely,
and, here it was that fate took Morag's hand.

On stepping stones she crossed the tumbling river,
and, rising up to crest a gentle hill,
she stopped, and, there before her in a valley
was a sight that made the kindly lady thrill.
A tiny figure, about two feet tall, thought Morag,
was pacing to and fro as on parade,
while, on a tiny set of martial bagpies
the finest stirring melodies he played.
Morag watched, enthralled, for several minutes
until, at last, the player stopped and smiled,
on seeing Morag, bowed and walked towards her
as Morag stood and waited, quite beguiled.

"Good day dear lady" said the tiny fellow.
"Good day" said Morag, "Please Oh! Please play more!
you play with such a style and such emotion
in a way that I have never heard before"
The tiny fellow smiled again, eyes sparkling,
"It is really very simple don't you see?
I live among the goblins, elves and faeries,
and, your children, every one, believe in me!
If they did not, though here, you'd never see me,
those stirring tunes I play you'd never hear,
that you may see and hear us when we're near"
Morag thought of Hamish, and, now laughing

asked the little man if he could aid
the residents who lived around Dunvegan,
by helping Hamish in the way he played.
Thus it was, that Hamish was made welcome
by everyone and all throught the land,
even playing at the castle of Barmoral
for the Royal Family at the Queen's command!
Pay no heed if someone says there are no faeries,
we know there are, suffice it that we do,
and just as long as we go on believing,
we will see our dearest hopes and dreams come true.

Octopusicality

An octopus is thought by us
as being somewhat scary,
and, when bathing in the sea
we all feel rather wary,
lest upon an octopus
we stumble, and, a dreadful fuss
would then ensue,
the water turn an inky blue
and, flee we would in such a state
from tentacles that number eight!
But, pause awhile and think of this,
our attitude could be amiss,
a gentler creature you will not find,
at least of the tentacular kind.
The widest smile, though let me state
it can, at times, intimidate
those of a nervous disposition.
Then, sad to say, in this condition
we seldom stay to have a chat,
of matters deep, or this and that.
But if you do, and then departure take,
remember, there will be eight hands to shake!

Brother Rabbit

I have never said much about rabbits,
to be honest, I can not say why,
but, when they start twitching their tiny wee noses,
I know not to laugh or to cry!
To laugh, for I find them enchanting,
they certainly captivate me.
To cry, for I know they have already eaten
my lettuce for afternoon tea!

A Polar Experience

I truely do not think I'd like
to be a polar bear,
though I do admit I envy them
the woolly coat they wear!
They always look so confident
relaxed and in control,
in fact, a little haughty
as, across the ice they stroll.
I admire them, and I would so love
their grandeur to aquire,
but, on second thoughts, I think
I'll stay here snugly by the fire,
until the winter passes and
when summer comes once more,
I rub my hand on silver sand
on a warm and sun kissed shore.

Ambition

I once knew a seagull, called Simon Mackay,
whose ambition in life was to sing.
Not to croak, or to squawk, like the rest of his kind,
but to sound like a lark on the wing.
He tried pursing his beak, as he saw children do
by the harbour whilst whistling a tune,
but, I'm rather afraid that the sound that he made
was akin to a mournful bassoon!
One day by the shore, as he practiced once more,
some sandpipers chanced to pass by,
and, hearing the deep sound that Simon was making
stopped, were silent, then loudly did cry,
'A deep rhythmic bass is just what is needed
to anchor our lighter toned choir'
and so from that day, Simon could say
he fulfilled his life's greatest desire.
They performed on the shore, on the pier, in the town,
as they did, their fame spread far and wide,
with Simon fulfilling his lifelong ambition,
performing with musical pride!

A Noble Rescue

The seagull sat atop the castle wall,
his wings spread, drying in the morning sun.
Below him, little figures stretched and rose,
for, in the castle, work had just begun.
The king, a mouse of sleek majestic brown,
had risen with his queen, of softer shade,
and, in the private room of their princess,
a gentle hand upon her head was laid.
A pretty little mouse, quite clearly loved
and cherished as their own by everyone,
the happiest of mice that sun-filled day,
little knowing an adventure had begun.

A gentle wind blew warmly from the sea
that lapped against the castle from the west,
and here she kept a sturdy little craft,
as sailing was the hobby she loved best.
After breakfast, the young princess made her way
to where a fine strong jetty held the sea
to leave a calm and tranquil little pool,
a favoured spot, one where she liked to be.
She deftly loosed the ties that held the craft
and, nimbly boarding, raised the little sail.
The breeze quite quickly filled it, and she rode
the rising waves, the wind now at her tail.
The seagull, from his lofty perch had watched
the tiny vessel sailing from the shore,
and, with keen eye, looking to the west,
tried to fathom what the weather had in store.

His eyes grew troubled, for the wind had swung
from west to south, now from the east did blow
gusting, then dropping, gusting once again,
foretelling danger to the craft below.
By now the princess, far out in the sea
having seen the danger, turned the ship around -
too late! she looked up terrified, and saw
the mast break, with a loud and fearful sound!
The tiny craft, completely helpless, lay
pitching and tossing on the raging billow.
The princess clutched the sides in great alarm.
Oh! how she longed for her warm bed and pillow
that such a little time ago she left,
and now, quite clearly, she in danger lay.
No one could hear her cries she felt quite sure,
no other sail in sight to save her day.

The seagull, from his perch, had watched the scene
and, now flew down from that great castle wall,
gliding and swooping through the open doors
he came to rest within the king's Great Hall.
The king, in robes of gold, sat on his throne,
his queen beside him, regal yet demure.
'This bird would not dare enter' she declared
'lest something is amiss, of that I'm sure'
The seagull nodded as he heard the mouse,
but, finding it impossible to speak,
he nodded to the couple with his head
and gestured to the door, with wings and beak.

The royals, then the courtiers, followed on,
running, to keep pace with the anxious bird,
then, as they reached the little harbour wall,
faintly, on the wind, a cry they heard.

'Our princess ' the queen cried out in despair,
'to rescue her must be our first concern'
The mice ran to and fro in such alarm,
but in truth, they knew not where to turn.
Siezing a length of rope in his stout beak,
the seagull beat his wings against the wind,
rose high overhead, and set his course
to where he hoped the stricken ship to find.

The princess was now tearful, wet and cold,
as wilder grew the sea, and she afraid
but, firmly did she cling to the ship's side
for, help will come, an inner voice had said.
A dangling rope then gently touched her cheek,
Looking up she saw the seagull overhead.
Quickly she took the rope and made it fast,
as into the wind the seagull turned and fled,
powering his wings against the howling gale
with beating heart, as strongly as he knew,
drawing her ever closer to the shore,
but weaker now, lower and lower flew.

At last the castle walls came into sight,
closer the harbour bar, then, in a trice
were bird and princess safely on the shore,
greeted by cheering from the gathered mice.
Much later, in the castle's echoing hall,
seagull was called before the royal pair.
As all the courtiers smiled and clapped and cheered,
this hero, who had saved their princess fair.

Then, stood the king, and silent fell the throng.
"Seagull, let me grant your dearest wish."
The seagull paused and thought, then replied
'Your majesty, the royal grant to fish
along this shore, from let and hindrance free'.
"So shall you have it" loudly cried the king
"henceforth shall you be Monarch of the sea."

Meercat Hill

Two meercats sat on meercat hill
viewing the far horizon.
A flock of haughty ostriches
was what they had their eyes on.
Close by, a lioness with cubs
were watching carefully
as, father lion, silently
stalked, before the birds could flee.
The alarm was raised,
with thundering feet,
the ostriches all fled,
save for the leader of the flock
who simply put his head
into a hole dug in the sand,
where motionless he stood,
whilst the racing lion
pursued his feathered food.
He ignored the senior ostrich,
completely passed him by,
and, one meercat asked the other,
"Please, can you tell me why?
Is it that he is old and wise,
experienced enough?"
"Let us just say, if he can't run away
he is old, and far too tough!"

Diversion

Robert was a rabbit,
with the most endearing habit
of visiting his grandma
every single day.
In a little house and garden,
and he requires no pardon,
after taking tea with grandma
in the garden he would play.
When the night had drawn in fully,
grandma told him that a bully
of a rabbit on a scooter,
on the road outside would stray.
The late hour he was keeping
meant, that grandma was not sleeping,
and, when Robert came a calling
dozed the afternoon away!

Robert felt quite heated,
this buck must be unseated
and Robert would approach the task
as subtly as he may.
Two lamps were there to guide you
with the billowing sea beside you,
whilst the road turned sharply to the left,
in safety you would stay.
When night fell, he astutely
moved the lamps minutely,
staying in his grandma's house
until the break of day.

Next morning, waking up before
his Gran, and, running to the shore,
saw the scooter in deep water-
Oh! so silently it lay!
He later heard another
buck, was punished by his mother
for returning home, quite soaking wet,
from being out to play!

Sticky

At breakfast time young oswald ant
was a terrible disgrace.
Crumbs and sticky marmalade
all over the breakfast place.
His mother was beside herself,
what was she to do?
When a friend of hers suggested,
"buy a tube of glue."
She spread it on the chair on which
that messy eater sat,
carefully avoiding it
being sat on by the cat!
Next morning, after breakfast,
Oswald gave a fearful shout!
"I'm stuck here in my chair Mama!
I simply can't get out!"
"The marmalade you splash about
has stuck you to your chair"
his mother said. Young Oswald cried,
'It really isn't fair!'
He left his favourite trousers there
-it did seem such a waste-
and, as he changed, and left for school
in such a frantic haste,
young Oswald could be heard to say
'there's a price that must be paid;
no more a messy eater,
no more spilt marmalade.

With my thanks to Ryan and Kathrin
Without whom this book would not have been possible.